Who would kill a skunk?

Corby Briggs stepped into the Brown Detective Agency. "What do you think of skunks?" he asked.

"I've got nothing against them," answered Encyclopedia, who felt it was important to let people know how he stood on issues. "They leave me alone. I leave them alone."

"Would you mind if your neighbor kept a skunk as a pet?" asked Corby.

"I don't know . . ." admitted Encyclopedia. "Living near skunks is something else."

"You can say that again," agreed Sally.

Corby took a quarter from his pocket. He laid it on the gasoline can beside Encyclopedia.

"I want you to find out who killed my pet skunk Buttercup this morning," he said.

Read all the books in the Encyclopedia Brown series!

No. 1 Encyclopedia Brown Boy Detective

No. 2 Encyclopedia Brown and the Case of the Secret Pitch

No. 3 Encyclopedia Brown Finds the Clues

No. 4 Encyclopedia Brown Gets His Man

No. 5 Encyclopedia Brown Solves Them All

No. 6 Encyclopedia Brown Keeps the Peace

No. 7 Encyclopedia Brown Saves the Day

No. 8 Encyclopedia Brown Tracks Them Down

No. 9 Encyclopedia Brown Shows the Way

No. 10 Encyclopedia Brown Takes the Case

No. 11 Encyclopedia Brown Lends a Hand

No. 12 Encyclopedia Brown and the Case of the Dead Eagles

No. 13 Encyclopedia Brown and the Case of the Midnight Visitor

Encyclopedia Brown

No. 10

Brown

Takes the
Case

By DONALD J. SOBOL

illustrated by Leonard Shortall

PUFFIN BOOKS

Published by the Penguin Group

Penguin Young Readers Group, 345 Hudson Street, New York, New York 10014, U.S.A.

Penguin Group (Canada), 90 Eglinton Avenue East, Suite 700,
Toronto, Ontario, Canada M4P 2Y3 (a division of Pearson Penguin Canada Inc.)

Penguin Books Ltd, 80 Strand, London WC2R 0RL, England

Penguin Ireland, 25 St Stephen's Green, Dublin 2, Ireland (a division of Penguin Books Ltd)

Penguin Group (Australia), 250 Camberwell Road, Camberwell, Victoria 3124, Australia
(a division of Pearson Australia Group Pty Ltd)

Penguin Books India Pvt Ltd, 11 Community Centre,
Panchsheel Park, New Delhi - 110 017, India

Penguin Group (NZ), 67 Apollo Drive, Rosedale, North Shore 0632, New Zealand
(a division of Pearson New Zealand Ltd)

Penguin Books (South Africa) (Pty) Ltd, 24 Sturdee Avenue,
Rosebank, Johannesburg 2196, South Africa

Registered Offices: Penguin Books Ltd, 80 Strand, London WC2R 0RL, England

First published in the United States of America by Dutton Children's Books,
a division of Penguin Young Readers Group, 1973
Published by Puffin Books, a division of Penguin Young Readers Group, 2008

10

THE LIBRARY OF CONGRESS HAS CATALOGED
THE DUTTON CHILDREN'S BOOKS EDITION AS FOLLOWS:
Sobol, Donald J.
Encyclopedia Brown takes the case.
(His Encyclopedia Brown book no. 10)
Summary: Idaville's secret weapon against law-breakers, ten-year-old Encyclopedia Brown
assists the police force with ten insoluble cases. Solutions are at the back of the book.
ISBN: 0-525-66318-5 (hc)
[1. Detective stories] I. Shortall, Leonard W., illus. II. Title.
PZ7.S68524Et [Fic] 73-6443

Puffin Books ISBN 978-0-14-241085-1

Printed in the United States of America

For
Marilyn and Murray Winston

Contents

1. *The Case of the Stolen Money*   11
2. *The Case of the Talking House*   19
3. *The Case of the Two-Timers*   26
4. *The Case of the False Teeth*   33
5. *The Case of the Skin Diver*   41
6. *The Case of the Barefoot Thieves*   48
7. *The Case of the Dog-Paddle Derby*   56
8. *The Case of the Broken Globe*   64
9. *The Case of the Pet Skunk*   72
10. *The Case of the Seven-Foot Driver*   79

Encyclopedia Brown

Takes the Case

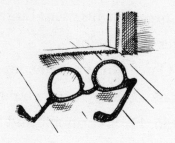

The Case of the Stolen Money

Police officers across America were asking the same question.

Why did everyone who broke the law in Idaville get caught?

Idaville looked like many seaside towns its size. It had two delicatessens, three movie theaters, and four banks. It had churches, a synagogue, and lovely white beaches. And it had a certain red brick house on Rover Avenue.

In the house lived Idaville's secret weapon against lawbreakers—ten-year-old Encyclopedia Brown.

Mr. Brown was chief of the Idaville police force. He was proud of his men. But he was not too proud to get them help.

Whenever Chief Brown came up against a case that no one on the force could solve, he knew what to do. He went home and ate dinner.

Before the meal was over, Encyclopedia had solved the case for him.

Chief Brown wanted to tell the world about his only child—to announce over satellite television, "My son is the greatest detective who ever shot a water pistol!"

But what good would it do? Who would believe that the mastermind behind Idaville's spotless police record was only a fifth-grader?

Encyclopedia never let slip a word about the help he gave his father. He didn't want to seem different from other boys his age.

But there was nothing he could do about his nickname.

Only his parents and teachers called him by

his real name, Leroy. Everyone else called him Encyclopedia.

An encyclopedia is a book or set of books filled with facts from A to Z—just like Encyclopedia's head. He had read more books than anyone in Idaville, and he never forgot what he read. His pals swore that if he went to sleep before thinking out a problem, he stuck a bookmark in his mouth.

Not all his father's most difficult cases happened in Idaville. Friday evening, for instance, the dinner table conversation turned to a mystery in another town.

"Bill Carleton, the Hills Grove chief of police, telephoned me this morning," said Chief Brown. "He has a robbery on his hands that's got him worried."

"Isn't Hills Grove up in Canada, dear?" asked Mrs. Brown.

"It's in northern Canada," answered Chief Brown. "Even during the summer the temperature sometimes drops below freezing."

"The Idaville police department is certainly famous," said Mrs. Brown proudly. "Imagine a call for help from Canada!"

"What was stolen, Dad?" asked Encyclopedia.

"Ten thousand dollars," said Chief Brown. "The money was taken three days ago from the safe in the home of Mr. and Mrs. Arthur Richter."

Chief Brown put down his soup spoon.

"I have all the facts from Chief Carleton," he said. "But I'm afraid I still can't help him find the thief."

"Tell Leroy," urged Mrs. Brown. "He's never failed you yet."

Chief Brown grinned at his son. "Are you ready?" he asked, taking a notebook from his breast pocket. He read what he had written down.

"*Last Friday Mr. and Mrs. Richter, who have lived in Hills Grove three years, flew to Detroit for the weekend. Before leaving, they gave a key*

He had just stepped through the front door when he
heard a noise in the study.

to their empty house to a friend, Sidney Auk-land, in case of an emergency. On Saturday, Aukland entered the house."

"Was it an emergency?" asked Mrs. Brown.

"No," replied Chief Brown. "The weather had turned cold. It had dropped below freezing. Aukland said he wanted to be sure there was enough heat in the house."

Chief Brown read again from his notebook.

"Aukland said he entered the house Saturday morning at ten o'clock. He had just stepped through the front door when he heard a noise in the study.

"He called out, 'Who's there?' and opened the study door. Two men were at the safe. They attacked him. He says he didn't have a chance once they knocked off his eyeglasses. Without them, he can't see six inches in front of himself.

"The two men tied him up, he says. It wasn't until an hour later that he worked himself free and called the police."

"Did Mr. Aukland get a look at the two men

while he still wore his eyeglasses?" asked Mrs. Brown.

"Yes," replied Chief Brown. "He says that if he sees them again, he'll recognize them."

"Then what is the mystery?" exclaimed Mrs. Brown. "Why did Chief Carleton telephone you for help, dear?"

"He suspects Aukland," said Chief Brown. "He thinks Aukland stole the money and made up the part about the two men. But he can't prove Aukland is lying."

Mrs. Brown glanced at Encyclopedia. As yet the boy detective had not asked his one question —the question that always enabled him to break a case.

Encyclopedia had finished his soup. He was sitting with his eyes closed. He always closed his eyes when he did his hardest thinking.

Suddenly his eyes opened.

"What was the temperature in the house, Dad?" he asked.

Chief Brown looked at his notebook.

"*Aukland says that the house was comfortably warm when he entered it. After finding his eyeglasses and calling the police, he checked the reading. It was seventy degrees.*"

"Leroy . . ." murmured Mrs. Brown. Disappointment was in her voice.

She was so proud when Encyclopedia solved a mystery for his father before she served the main course. But sometimes she had to wait until dessert. This looked like a dessert case.

"What is important about heat?" she asked.

"Not any heat, Mom," said Encyclopedia. "The heat in the house."

"I don't follow you, son," said Chief Brown.

"The house was too hot for Mr. Aukland to have seen two men robbing the safe," answered Encyclopedia. "He made them up."

HOW DID ENCYCLOPEDIA KNOW?

(*Turn to page 87 for the solution to The Case of the Stolen Money.*)

The Case of the Talking House

Encyclopedia helped his father solve mysteries throughout the year. In the summer, he helped the neighborhood children as well.

When school let out, he opened his own detective agency in the garage. Every morning he hung out his sign.

BROWN DETECTIVE AGENCY
13 Rover Avenue
Leroy Brown, President
No case too small
25¢ per day
plus expenses

His first customer Monday afternoon was Scoop McGinnis.

Scoop was five. He could neither read nor write. But with the help of his older sister, he put out a two-page weekly newspaper, *The Cricket*.

The Cricket was by kids, for kids, and about kids. It stood for good citizenship, zoos, toys, and better hot dogs. It was against bad candy and people who didn't like *The Cricket*.

When he came to see Encyclopedia, Scoop was sucking his forefinger.

Right away Encyclopedia knew something was wrong. Scoop usually sucked his thumb.

"You know the old Webster house on the beach?" asked Scoop.

Encyclopedia knew it. No one had lived there for years and years. The window glass had fallen out. Six inches of sand covered the floors.

"The house is so old it's dangerous," said Encyclopedia. "The city plans to knock it down next week."

"That house was mad," said Scoop. "It bited me."

"You mean it *bit* you," corrected Encyclopedia. Then he caught himself. "Houses don't bite!"

"Look at my finger," said Scoop.

Encyclopedia looked. "You've got a splinter," he said.

Scoop frowned. "If that house didn't bite me, then maybe it didn't talk to me."

"Keep calm," Encyclopedia told himself. "I was once five years old myself."

To Scoop he said, "Would you mind starting at the beginning, please?"

"This morning after breakfast, I interviewed that house for *The Cricket*," said Scoop. "I wanted to know how it felt about being knocked down."

"That's when it bit you?"

"That's when it talked to me," said Scoop. "It said it takes a lot of money to save a house. It told me to go home and bring all my money. I did—a dollar and fifty cents."

"It wasn't enough," guessed Encyclopedia.

"How did you know?" said Scoop. "Because I didn't bring more, the house got mad and bit me—I thought. I dropped the money and ran."

"Were you alone in the house?" inquired Encyclopedia.

Scoop shook his head. "As I was running out, I saw a big kid in the next room trying to hide. I think it was Bugs Meany."

"Bugs!" exclaimed Encyclopedia. "I might have known he was mixed up in this!"

Bugs Meany was the leader of the Tigers, a gang of tough older boys. Encyclopedia was often called upon to stop their dishonest doings.

Only last week he had put a halt to the Tigers' "Giant Summer Pet Sale." Bugs had dipped seven sparrows in peroxide and tried to sell them as canaries.

"Can you get back my money?" asked Scoop. "I'll have to pay you later."

"Don't worry about it," said Encyclopedia. He took out Scoop's splinter, and the two

Bugs lay on the porch. He was scratching his dandruff and picking his teeth.

boys set off for the old beach house.

"Bugs must have seen you run away," Encyclopedia told Scoop. "He knew you were heading to see me. He's probably waiting for us—with an alibi!"

Encyclopedia was right. Bugs lay on the porch. He was scratching his dandruff and picking his teeth. When he saw the boy detective, he sat up quickly.

"Scram, or your face will need help," he snarled.

Encyclopedia was used to Bugs's warm welcomes. He nodded and went inside with Scoop. Bugs followed them.

Scoop stopped among the many footprints in the deep sand that covered the living-room floor.

"I started to put the dollar and a half on that shelf," he said. "Then the splinter bit me. I got scared. I dropped the money and ran."

Encyclopedia studied the large cracks in the walls. "Bugs could have stood in the next room, watching and listening," he said.

"What's with you two crazy cats?" demanded

Bugs. "I came here for some wood. I'm adding a poolroom to the Tigers' clubhouse."

"You made me think the house was talking," said Scoop. "You took my money."

"I didn't take anything except a nap," said Bugs. "The wood in this dump wouldn't make a good slop bucket."

He began walking slowly around the room.

"Your money is still here if you *really* dropped it," he declared. "You shouldn't go around accusing people of stealing. There are laws against that sort of thing."

Suddenly he gave a cry and pointed.

In the sand on the floor lay a half dollar. Under it was a dollar bill.

"G-gosh, Bugs," stammered Scoop. "I thought the worst of you. I'm sorry."

"Don't be," said Encyclopedia. "If you hadn't run out of the room and seen Bugs, he'd have kept your money!"

WHAT MADE ENCYCLOPEDIA SO CERTAIN?

(Turn to page 88 for the solution to The Case of the Talking House.)

The Case of the Two-Timers

If Bugs Meany had a goal in life, it was to get even with Encyclopedia.

Bugs hated being outsmarted all the time. He longed to sock the boy detective on the side of his face so hard that he could look down his back without turning his head.

But Bugs never threw the punch. Whenever he felt like it, he remembered a pair of lightning-fast fists.

The fists belonged to Sally Kimball, Encyclopedia's partner. Sally was the prettiest girl in the fifth grade as well as the best athlete. And she had done what no boy under twelve had dreamed possible.

She had out-punched Bugs Meany.

Every time they had come to blows, Bugs had ended on the ground, mumbling about falling rocks.

Because of Sally, Bugs was afraid to use muscle on Encyclopedia. However, he never stopped planning his day of revenge.

"Bugs hates you as much as he hates me," Encyclopedia warned Sally. "He won't ever forgive you for showing him up."

"I know," said Sally. "He's more like a magician than a Tiger. He can turn anything into trouble."

"Trouble," thought Encyclopedia, "may be where we are heading."

The detectives were walking in downtown Idaville. Half an hour earlier, Lefty Dobbs had telephoned them. Lefty had said to meet him in front of the city hall right away.

"I wonder why Lefty didn't tell you what this

is all about," remarked Sally.

"Perhaps he couldn't talk freely over the telephone," replied Encyclopedia. "Anyway, we'll soon find out. There he is."

Lefty was standing outside the city hall. He saw the two detectives, but he didn't wave. Instead, he took off his wristwatch.

"He's acting awfully nervous," whispered Sally as they drew closer. "I don't trust him."

With his right hand, Lefty held his watch by the metal strap. Between his left forefinger and thumb he turned the tiny knob that set the time.

As he did, he checked the big clock atop the city hall. It showed five minutes before three.

"Are you okay?" Encyclopedia asked him.

"Sssh!" hissed Lefty. "Keep your voice down."

"What's the big secret?" asked Sally.

"Show me your palm, Encyclopedia," said Lefty.

Encyclopedia held out his hand, palm upward.

Lefty laid twenty-five cents on it. "I want to hire you," he said.

"There! You saw it yourself, officer!"

For a moment he stared up at the clock atop the city hall with a thoughtful expression. Then he fished into his pocket and took out a five-dollar bill. He gave it to Encyclopedia.

"This case is extra tough," he whispered. "So I'll pay more."

"*There! You saw it yourself, officer!*"

It was Bugs Meany. He came charging out of a nearby dress shop. Behind him was Officer Hall.

"I told you we'd catch them in the act, the little crooks!" cried Bugs.

"You'd better have an explanation," Officer Hall said to the detectives. "I saw everything through these binoculars Bugs lent me."

"They've been working this racket for weeks," said Bugs.

"What racket?" gasped Sally, bewildered.

"Bugs told me that you wait until some child stops to set his watch by the time on the city-hall clock," said Officer Hall. "Then you approach him. You tell him the price for setting his watch is twenty-five cents."

"Encyclopedia told me he owned the clock," put in Lefty.

Bugs had been shaking his head sadly as he listened. Now he clasped his hands over his chest and put on a righteous face.

"So many kids came to me with complaints," he said. "I knew it was my duty as a good citizen to go to the police. Of course, I hated doing it. I'm so sensitive, so high-strung."

"You ought to be strung higher," snapped Sally. "This is nothing but a frame-up!"

"It's serious," corrected Officer Hall. "I saw money change hands."

"I paid Encyclopedia a quarter for setting my watch," said Lefty. "Then he sold me the collection rights for five dollars. He said I'd make ten dollars a week easy collecting twenty-five cents from every watch setter."

"You poor innocent slob," said Bugs. "Encyclopedia doesn't own the clock. You've been cheated."

"I—I can't believe it!" exclaimed Lefty. "Encyclopedia Brown a common thief! Can you get back my money, Bugs?"

"The law takes care of his kind," said Bugs, patting Officer Hall on the shoulder. "Don't worry. Your money will be returned."

Sally was beside herself with rage. "You don't really *believe* them?" she protested to Officer Hall. "They're lying! This is nothing but a plot to get us in trouble. Didn't you *hear* what was said?"

"I couldn't hear from inside the dress shop," admitted the policeman. "But I saw everything clearly while Bugs explained what was going on."

"I'm sure he did a very good job," said Encyclopedia, "except for . . ."

FOR WHAT?

(*Turn to page 89 for the solution to The Case of the Two-Timers.*)

The Case of the False Teeth

Sunday afternoon, Encyclopedia and Sally went to the beach. They took a football. They should have taken a kite.

A strong wind was sweeping in from the ocean. It blew their tosses into palm trees and sunbathers.

"I'm tired of dirty looks," said Sally. "Let's build something."

"We can build an atom smasher," said Encyclopedia.

They put aside the football and dug in the sand. The atom smasher was nearly finished when

33

Freddy put down the jar he was carrying. Inside it were several sets of false teeth.

it was smashed. Freddy Zacharias walked right through it.

Freddy worked hard all summer combing the beaches. He collected the rare bottles and shells which his father sold at his gift shop on Ocean-front Drive.

"I'm sorry," Freddy apologized. "I wasn't looking where I was going."

"Never mind," said Encyclopedia. "We've had our fun. You're lucky we didn't build a hole."

"So am I," said Freddy. "If I'd fallen in, I might have bitten myself all over."

"What did you say?" asked Encyclopedia.

Freddy put down the jar he was carrying. Inside it were several sets of false teeth.

"During the week I help my father," he said. "On Sundays, I'm in business for myself."

Encyclopedia stared at the jar. He tried not to imagine Freddy stealing up on sunbathers and slipping out their false teeth while they slept.

"I find them in the shallows," said Freddy.

"Sunday is always the best day. False teeth that get lost off Key South take a week to be carried north to Idaville."

Key South was a big fishing and vacation area, and cruise ships put in there on Sundays. Freddy explained that lots of false teeth were lost overboard by tourists and fishermen. Others were jarred loose from swimmers' mouths by waves.

"The *Idaville News* prints ads for lost teeth," he said. "Usually, there is a reward."

He showed the detectives two ads he had clipped from the newspaper. Each promised a reward for the return of teeth lost over the past weekend.

"I measure the teeth I find and write to the people who place the ads," said Freddy. "So far this summer I've returned eight sets of teeth. The reward money paid for my new ten-speed bicycle."

"Hopping choppers!" exclaimed Encyclopedia. "Out of the mouths of grown-ups!"

"Don't just stand there, Freddy," urged Sally.

"Be on your way. Keep looking!"

"All right," said Freddy. "I'm really sorry about stepping on your sand thing."

He moved off down the beach, eyes on the surf line.

The detectives took a swim. The wind was still blowing in from the ocean as strongly as ever when they quit the water. They decided to build a bigger atom smasher.

They had just begun when Freddy came running up.

"Some kids stole my teeth!" he cried.

"Who?" asked Encyclopedia.

"Two Tigers, Duke Kelly and Rocky Graham," replied Freddy. He was about to break into tears.

"The big goons," said Sally, clenching her fists. "When I catch them, they'll need false teeth themselves!"

"Maybe we can get back your teeth, Freddy," said Encyclopedia calmly. "Let's go talk with Duke and Rocky."

As they headed down the beach, Freddy related what had happened.

Duke Kelly had snatched the jar as he had walked past. When the two Tigers saw what was inside, they laughed and took out the teeth. Duke went into a Spanish dance, stomping and whirling and clicking teeth like castanets.

"Duke got careless," said Freddy. "As he was clicking and stomping and whirling, he swung his hands too close to his head. He bit himself in the right ear."

"Serves him right!" said Sally.

"It made him awful sore at me," said Freddy. "He kicked over the jar and the ads flew out. Rocky caught them and read them to Duke. They told me to beat it."

"They're hoping to get the rewards themselves!" exclaimed Sally. "We'd better hurry."

"There's Duke under that palm tree," said Encyclopedia.

Duke was lying in the shade, holding his sore ear. Neither Rocky nor the jar was in sight.

"Rocky's probably taken the teeth back to the Tigers' clubhouse," said Sally.

Duke saw them approaching. He sat up, watching Sally uneasily.

"Where's Rocky?" inquired Encyclopedia.

"He went home," said Duke. "Too much sunburn."

"You stole Freddy's false teeth," Sally accused. "Give them back!"

"Stole . . . ?" cried Duke. "After all I did for him, he accuses me of stealing?"

"Just what have you done for him?" said Encyclopedia.

"He was walking past me with a jar under his arm," said Duke. "Suddenly he tripped. A couple of newspaper clippings fell out, and some false teeth."

"The teeth bit your ear, I suppose," said Sally.

"Naw, the clippings blew into the ocean," said Duke. "I tried to save them and stumbled. I fell with my head under water. A crab bit me.

When I needed help, where was your Freddy?
Running off with his jar!"

"Sorry, Duke," said Encyclopedia. "You
tried, but you blew it!"

WHAT WAS DUKE'S MISTAKE?

*(Turn to page 90 for the solution to The Case of the False
Teeth.)*

The Case of the Skin Diver

When Encyclopedia and Sally went fishing in Mill Pond, they got there early in the morning before anyone else.

But Friday morning they weren't the earliest. As they arrived, Trisk Ford was climbing up the slope from the pond. He was moaning.

"Where do you hurt?" asked Sally, hurrying to his side.

"In my calendar," said Trisk. "Don't you know what day this is?"

"Friday," said Sally.

"Friday the *thirteenth*," corrected Trisk,

41

whose real name was Bruce. Trisk was short for triskaidekaphobe, which means someone who is afraid of the number 13.

"I don't believe in unlucky numbers," said Sally. "It's plain silly."

"Is it?" said Trisk. "When was the last time you saw a building with a thirteenth floor? If a black cat crosses your path today, you better hop on the nearest bus."

"Even if I don't have a fur piece to go?" said Sally.

"It's no joke," said Trisk. "Five minutes ago I nearly got a terrible pain in my neck."

He explained. He had awakened at sunrise. Rather than spend the day in the closet, he had decided to hide in the fresh air.

"I walked down to the pond," he said. "But I got bored sitting in the bushes. I started scaling stones on the water. Suddenly I saw something shining on the ground. It was a gold earring."

"Golly," said Encyclopedia. "I'll bet it's the one Mrs. Adams lost at the Girl Scout picnic last month. Where is it?"

"I was holding it when a mean kid stepped out of the bushes," said Trisk. "He stole it. Then he chopped the air with his hand and said, 'Scram, or I'll give you a double chin in the back of your neck.' "

"What did he look like?" asked Encyclopedia.

"I couldn't tell," answered Trisk. "He had on a glass face mask."

"Well, what was he wearing?"

"I just told you," said Trisk. "A face mask. He must have been going skin diving in only his skin."

"How old was he?" said Sally. "What was the color of his hair?"

"He was about twelve," replied Trisk. "He had brown hair, parted down the middle."

"He's probably all dressed by now," said Encyclopedia. "But if we hurry, we might catch him."

The three children ran down the slope. The pond was half a mile long, and the shore curved and twisted with hiding places. For a minute they saw no one.

"I was holding the earring when a mean kid stepped out of the bushes," said Trisk.

"There he is!" exclaimed Encyclopedia.

A boy, fully clothed, had appeared from some bushes a few yards away. He carried a face mask and a towel.

"It's that good-for-nothing Marlin Hayes," said Sally.

Marlin was a lazy seventh-grader. Last year his father wanted him to take a summer job cutting lawns. Instead, Marlin took up karate, the better to fight working.

"It couldn't have been Marlin," said Trisk. "His hair is the same color, but it's parted on the side."

"So it is . . ." observed Sally.

Nevertheless, she ran up to Marlin and gripped him by the arm. "You stole an earring from Trisk," she said. "Give it back!"

"Sally—p-please," gasped Encyclopedia. He had seen karate experts chop boards in half, bare-handed.

"I know you," said Marlin, looking down his nose. "You're the little chick who has the Tigers scared cuckoo. And you're Mr. Know-it-all.

And you must be the kid who wears earrings."

Trisk reddened. His hands clenched, but all he held was his tongue.

Sally wasn't so easily frightened. "You stole the earring while you were walking to the water to skin dive," she said to Marlin.

"Your head is out of town," Marlin retorted. "I was skin diving when this kid started scaling stones. One nearly hit me. So I came ashore and asked him to stop."

"If you're innocent, you won't care if we search you," said Encyclopedia.

"Right on," said Marlin with an amused smile. "I'll help."

He turned the pockets of his pants and shirt inside out. They held a dollar bill, two nickels, and a dirty handkerchief.

Sally's eyes narrowed.

"Stay out of it, Encyclopedia," she said softly. "I can solve this case myself."

She turned back to Marlin. "You hid the earring because you saw us talking with Trisk. Where is it?"

"I'm trying not to get angry," said Marlin. "But keep accusing me of stealing, and I might change my mind."

"Change it. It'll work better," said Sally.

"Now you've gone too far!" announced Marlin.

He circled Sally, shouting fighting words and moving his hands like ax blades.

"He'll chop her to pieces with his karate!" squeaked Trisk.

Sally, however, didn't give him the chance. She peppered him with jabs and crossed a right to the jaw. Marlin's eyes squinched shut in pain.

"Ooooo . . . enough!" he wailed. "Stop!" He held his head and looked at Sally fearfully.

"How'd you know?" he gasped. "What made you so *sure* I stole the earring?"

WHAT?

(Turn to page 91 for the solution to The Case of the Skin Diver.)

The Case of the Barefoot Thieves

Tyrone Taylor knew how to treat the fair sex.

He was the only boy in Idaville who got up to give a girl his seat—even when they were the only two passengers on the bus. The other fifth-grade boys called him Sir Galahad.

Monday afternoon Tyrone came into the Brown Detective Agency. He looked as sick as a horse.

"Don't call me Sir Galahad," he said sadly. "Call me Sir Had-a-Gal."

"Who was it this time?" asked Encyclopedia.

"Betty Holden," said Tyrone. "Just when I

figured I had a chance with her, what happens? She goes out with Stingy Stetson!"

"Don't worry," said Encyclopedia. "Stingy is so tight that if he blinks his eyes, his knuckles crack. When he dates a girl, the money flows like glue."

"That's what I thought," said Tyrone. "But last night I saw them together in Mr. O'Hara's drugstore. Stingy bought her the Idaville Special with *three* scoops of ice cream!"

"Wow! That costs twenty cents extra," exclaimed Encyclopedia.

"I want to hire you," said Tyrone. He slammed a quarter on the gasoline can beside Encyclopedia. "Find out where Stingy stole the money he's spending."

"Just a minute," said Encyclopedia. "You can't go around accusing him of stealing—"

"What was he doing outside the Medical Building yesterday morning?" snapped Tyrone. "It was Sunday. The building was closed. And you should have seen his crazy walk."

Encyclopedia scratched his head. "You'd better show me," he said.

The two boys biked to the Medical Building. It was after five o'clock when they arrived. The doctors had all gone home. The parking lot was empty.

"Sunday was a hot day," said Tyrone. "So I sat under that shade tree while I thought about Betty. Suddenly I saw Stingy and his big brother Pete. They were walking in the parking lot, one behind the other. Crazy!"

"Crazy?" repeated Encyclopedia.

"They walked as if they couldn't keep their balance," said Tyrone. "Then they jumped into a red truck that had 'Mac's Service Station' written on the door. They drove away, *zoom!*"

"Sit under the same tree," said Encyclopedia. "I'll do what they did."

He went down to the parking lot, which was enclosed by a seven-foot stone wall. He walked across the blacktop surface till he could see Tyrone over the wall.

"Stingy and Pete were farther back," said Tyrone. "I can see only your head above the wall. I saw them down to the waist."

Encyclopedia moved back a few steps.

"Stop," called Tyrone. "That's where they were."

Encyclopedia had halted on a long, narrow white line. Branching out on either side of it were short white lines to mark spaces for cars to park.

"Stingy and Pete were walking a narrow white line you can't see from there," shouted Encyclopedia. "They were having fun keeping their balance."

"Fun, nothing," insisted Tyrone. "They were celebrating. They probably just robbed some doctor's office."

Tyrone refused to believe anything but the worst about Stingy. He made Encyclopedia promise to ask his father if the Medical Building had been robbed yesterday.

At dinner, Encyclopedia put the question to his father.

"Why, yes," answered Chief Brown, surprised. "Officer Clancy handled the case. I learned about it this morning."

"What was stolen, dear?" asked Mrs. Brown.

"Thieves took about two hundred dollars altogether from the petty-cash boxes in several offices," said Chief Brown.

"Isn't the Medical Building locked on Sunday?" asked Encyclopedia.

"The front door lock was broken Saturday," said Chief Brown. "A watchman was hired till it could be repaired today."

"Where was the watchman during the robbery?" asked Mrs. Brown.

"He was drinking at the water fountain when he glimpsed two pairs of bare feet disappearing up the stairs," said Chief Brown. "He chased them. As he turned a corner, he was struck and knocked out. He awoke to see Mac's red service truck leave the parking lot."

"So the robbers work at Mac's gas station!" declared Mrs. Brown.

"We can't be sure," said Chief Brown. "The

*He was drinking at the water fountain when he glimpsed
two pair of bare feet disappearing up the stairs.*

watchman telephoned Mac immediately. Sundays the truck is driven by Pete Stetson. Sometimes he takes his younger brother—the one everyone calls Stingy—along on service calls. When they returned to the station, both boys had on shoes."

"What were the Stetson boys doing at the parking lot?" asked Mrs. Brown.

"Pete said he was looking for a key, which he thought he dropped Saturday after visiting Dr. Marshall. He did see the doctor. We checked on that."

Chief Brown took a spoonful of soup. Then he continued.

"No doubt the thieves removed their shoes in order to walk more quietly," he said. "Pete and Stingy may have robbed the offices. But we can't shake their alibi."

"You mean, you need a clue to prove they had their shoes off when they entered the building?" said Mrs. Brown.

"One clue will do," said Chief Brown. "But we don't have even one."

"I have," said Encyclopedia.

WHAT WAS THE CLUE?

(Turn to page 92 for the solution to The Case of the Barefoot Thieves.)

The Case of the Dog-Paddle Derby

Business kept Encyclopedia and Sally in the detective agency all morning. Not until noon were they free to bike to the rock pit, where the Idaville Dog-Paddle Derby was being held.

"If we hurry, we can see the final," said Encyclopedia.

Sally was upset. "A swimming meet in a rock pit!" she exclaimed. "Dogs should be allowed in pools."

"It's against the health law," said Encyclopedia.

"Why?" demanded Sally. "There are more

short-haired dogs than people."

"Maybe dogs won't swim in people-polluted pools," said Encyclopedia.

At the rock pit they were met by Fangs Live-right, one of Encyclopedia's pals. Pinned to his shirt was a button with the words "Meat Director."

"Shouldn't that be 'Meet Director'?" Sally asked.

"No, I'm in charge of the meat," said Fangs. "The winning dog gets five pounds of hamburger."

The three children walked through the crowd till they stood at the edge of the rock pit. It was filled with rainwater.

"Too bad you missed the heats," said Fangs. "The final is about to start. It's a sprint—just one lap."

"No lap dogs allowed, of course," commented Sally. "They'd have too big an advantage."

Encyclopedia watched five dogs being lined up by a teen-age boy. He was moving a cocker

*Encyclopedia watched five dogs being lined up by a
teen-age boy.*

spaniel into position. He had one hand under the dog's jaw.

"Who is he?" asked the boy detective.

"Horace Cushing, from the north side," said Fangs. "He's an official, like me and Puddinghead Peabody. Puddinghead is water boy."

Beside each dog was a one-quart bowl filled to the top with water. Fangs explained that Puddinghead emptied the bowls after each race and filled them before the next with fresh water from a can.

"Every dog gets the same, a full quart of water," said Fangs. "It's a hot day, and we don't want thirsty dogs. They might stop to drink during the race."

Encyclopedia nodded. He understood the importance of being fair to all the dogs. A lot was at stake. The winner would advance to the state championship.

"In this kind of race, it's easy to tell the underdog," observed Encyclopedia. "But who is the favorite?"

"Rags, the cocker spaniel," said Fangs. "Rags not only cleans his plate, but dries it with his ears."

"How many housewives can do that!" cried Sally.

Just then the starter's gun went off.

In an instant the five dogs were off and swimming. Or four were.

Rags, the favorite, had rolled over on his side. His tearful owner tried frantically to awaken him. In vain. Rags was still fast asleep when the race ended.

"What do you make of that?" gasped Sally.

"I'm afraid somebody fed him knockout drops to keep him from winning," replied Encyclopedia.

"How?" said Sally. "So many people are watching."

"Is there anyplace around here where someone can hide for a few minutes?" asked Encyclopedia.

"Over there," said Fangs. He pointed to a

large shed, which had been built when the rock pit was being worked. "There's a hose outlet on the other side of the shed. Puddinghead used it to fill his water can."

"Did Horace Cushing, the starter, ever go in there?" asked Sally.

"A couple of times," replied Fangs. "I'm pretty sure he was stealing a smoke."

Fangs paused thoughtfully.

"You know the dog that won the final?" he said. "He's owned by Horace. But come to think of it, the dog that finished second belongs to Puddinghead!"

"Either boy could have doped Rags to give his own dog a better chance," said Sally.

"You'll have to excuse me," said Fangs. "I'm supposed to award the hamburger meat to the winner."

Before he could walk away, Puddinghead came over.

"Here," he said, handing Fangs a shiny one-gallon gasoline can. "Thanks a lot."

"You used a *gasoline can* to fill the water bowls?" howled Sally.

"It's brand new," Fangs assured her. "My dad bought it this morning."

"Tell me something," said Encyclopedia. "When you filled the gasoline can with water before the final race, did you see anyone at the work shed?"

"Just Horace Cushing," answered Puddinghead. "He was grinding out a cigarette."

"Was he still there when you went back?" asked Encyclopedia.

"I wouldn't know," said Puddinghead. "I only made one trip for water. After I filled the bowls, I waited around for the race to begin."

After Puddinghead had left, Sally shook her head.

"Puddinghead couldn't have filled the gasoline can with water at the shed, put in the knockout drops, and filled all the bowls. Every dog in the race would have been knocked out. He has to be innocent."

"You mean he'd be innocent if this were Canada," replied Encyclopedia. "But this is Idaville, U.S.A."

WHAT DID ENCYCLOPEDIA MEAN?

(Turn to page 93 for the solution to The Case of the Dog-Paddle Derby.)

The Case of the Broken Globe

The Browns were sitting in the living room after dinner when Mr. Morton stopped by.

Mr. Morton taught at the high school. He and Chief Brown had been friends since boyhood.

"I hate to bother you at this hour," apologized Mr. Morton. "But . . . well, something serious happened in my class today."

He put down his briefcase and took a seat.

"I need your help . . . er . . . as a friend," he said.

"I understand," said Chief Brown. "You want to keep the trouble quiet."

"Yes," replied Mr. Morton. "My students aren't criminals. And to tell the truth, no law was broken."

"I promise not to make any arrests, if that is what is worrying you," said Chief Brown with a grin. "Now, what is this all about?"

"I gave my journalism class a test today," said Mr. Morton. "I left the room for five minutes. While I was gone, a globe of the world, worth ninety dollars, was smashed."

"And you want me to find out who broke it?" asked Chief Brown.

"I do," said Mr. Morton. "I doubt if it was knocked over on purpose. More likely, it was an accident. However, no one in the class will tell me who broke it."

"Everyone is afraid of being a squealer, eh?" said Chief Brown in annoyance. "Protect the guilty! I bump into that kind of foolishness every week."

"What was the test you gave the journalism class?" asked Mrs. Brown.

"It was on caption writing," answered Mr. Morton. "Each student was given six pictures and told to write a caption—a description—for each."

Mr. Morton opened his briefcase. He pulled out the test papers and showed them to Chief Brown.

Chief Brown looked at them quickly and handed them to Mrs. Brown. She gave each a glance and passed them to Encyclopedia.

While the grown-ups talked about the case, the boy detective gave the tests his full attention. Each student had been given the same pictures to work with. The difference in what each wrote was remarkable.

One of the test papers, turned in by a boy named Gene Dickman, caught Encyclopedia's eye. Whereas the other students had written captions of twenty to fifty words, Gene had written only one word under each picture.

Under a picture of a clock with both hands pointing to 12, he had written "NOON."

While the grown-ups talked about the case, the boy detective gave the tests his full attention.

Under a picture of an old sea captain scanning the horizon with a spyglass, he had written "SEES."

Under a picture of a screen with white dots, he had written "RADAR."

Under a picture of a calm and unrippled lake, he had written "LEVEL."

Under a picture of a paperhanger working on a wall, he had written "REPAPER."

Under a picture of a small airplane, he had written "SOLOS."

"I wonder . . ." Encyclopedia muttered.

Hurriedly he checked the names at the top of the other test papers: Robert Mason, Mary Keith, Anna McGill, George Worth, Mike Duval, Phil Johnson, Connie Logan, Scott Muncie, and Dwight Sherman.

Encyclopedia closed his eyes. He always closed his eyes when he did his heaviest thinking.

Then he asked a question. One question was all he needed to ask in order to solve a case.

"Are these all the students in your class, Mr. Morton?"

"Yes, it's a small class," answered the teacher. "There are three girls and seven boys."

Suddenly Mr. Morton frowned. He had noticed Gene Dickman's test papers on top of the pile on Encyclopedia's lap.

"I don't understand what happened to Gene," said Mr. Morton. "He is my brightest student, and yet he failed. He wrote only one word under each picture!"

"Perhaps he didn't have time to write more," said Chief Brown, "because he broke the globe."

Mr. Morton shook his head. "I left the classroom right after giving out the tests. I was gone only five minutes. Gene and everyone else had plenty of time to finish the test before the period ended."

"I thought you tried to find out who broke the globe," said Chief Brown. "Didn't that take time?"

"No," replied Mr. Morton. "I didn't notice the broken globe till the bell rang. I held the class a few minutes, but nobody confessed."

"It's a tough case," admitted Chief Brown. "There is no telling which boy is guilty."

"Maybe the guilty person is a girl," said Mrs. Brown.

"You're both right," said Encyclopedia. "A boy and a girl are guilty."

For a moment the room was quiet. The grown-ups stared in amazement at the boy detective.

"Leroy," said his mother. "How do you know that?"

"I learned it from Gene Dickman," replied Encyclopedia.

"You spoke with Gene . . . ?" gasped Mr. Morton.

"No, I read his test," replied Encyclopedia. "The way I see it, Gene didn't want to be called a squealer. But neither did he like seeing the guilty boy and girl refuse to own up to what they did."

"I don't understand a word," protested Mr. Morton.

"Gene used the test to name the guilty boy and girl," explained Encyclopedia.

HOW?

(Turn to page 94 for the solution to The Case of the Broken Globe.)

The Case of the Pet Skunk

Corby Briggs stepped into the Brown Detective Agency. "What do you think of skunks?" he asked.

"I've got nothing against them," answered Encyclopedia, who felt it was important to let people know how he stood on issues. "They leave me alone. I leave them alone."

"Would you mind if your neighbor kept a skunk as a pet?" asked Corby.

"I don't know . . ." admitted Encyclopedia. "Living near skunks is something else."

"You can say that again," agreed Sally. "One

or two skunks move in down the street. Then they bring their friends. The first thing you know, there goes the neighborhood!"

Corby took a quarter from his pocket. He laid it on the gasoline can beside Encyclopedia.

"I want you to find out who killed my pet skunk Buttercup this morning," he said.

"Killed?" gasped Sally. "Why, that's terrible!"

"Do you suspect anyone?" asked Encyclopedia. "Think hard. Who hated Buttercup enough to kill him?"

"I can't say," replied Corby. "None of the neighbors has spoken to me since I made him my pet."

Encyclopedia rose from his chair. "We'd better have a look at the scene of the crime," he said.

Corby lived three blocks farther down Rover Avenue. As they walked, he explained how he had taken up with a skunk.

Two weeks ago Buttercup had wandered out

of the woods, weak and lame. Corby had called the Humane Society. He had called the Animal Control. He had called the Coast Guard. But no one comes and gets skunks, he had discovered.

So he had put out food for the hungry animal. That was the start.

Every morning thereafter, Buttercup dropped by for a free meal when Corby fed his four cats and three dogs.

"Buttercup was especially fond of dry cat food," said Corby.

The children had reached Corby's house. He pointed to Buttercup's body.

"I haven't touched a thing," he said.

Buttercup lay near the back door, beside a bowl half filled with cat food. Encyclopedia examined the body. He could find neither blood nor bruises.

"We should bury him, poor thing," murmured Sally.

She and Corby set about the task while Encyclopedia examined the area. In a garbage can

Every morning Buttercup dropped by for a free meal when Corby fed his four dogs and four cats.

near the door he found what he sought—a bottle marked "poison." It was empty.

Beside the garbage can he found something else—a piece of notebook paper, the kind school-children use. On it was typewritten:

"In order to succeed you have to proceed to exceed."

Encyclopedia showed the paper to Corby.

"It's not mine," said Corby. "What does it mean? Is it a clue?"

"Maybe," said Encyclopedia. "It must have dropped from the guilty person's pocket when he pulled out the bottle of poison. Did you see anyone near the house this morning?"

"Jim Carnes, Bert Fenton, and Chuck Mitchell always cut through the yard on the way to summer school," said Corby. "I don't remember if I saw any of them this morning, though."

"Do they walk together?" asked Sally.

"No," replied Corby. "But sometimes they pass the house within five minutes of each other."

Encyclopedia knew the three boys. They were

taking makeup courses so they could be promoted to seventh grade in the fall.

"One of them could have poisoned Buttercup's food while he was eating and tossed the bottle into the garbage can," said Encyclopedia.

"Which one?" said Sally

"We'll have to go over to the school to learn that," said Encyclopedia.

Sally pressed him to explain. But Encyclopedia wasn't ready to discuss the case. He needed one more clue.

The eleven-o'clock classes had just begun when the three children reached the Idaville Elementary School. They went straight to the office.

Encyclopedia spoke with Mr. Pearlman, the assistant principal. He told him about the poisoning, and that he suspected Jim Carnes, or Bert Fenton, or Chuck Mitchell.

Mr. Pearlman listened, frowning. "But how can I help you?" he said.

"You could find out if one of the boys had to take a test this morning," said Encyclopedia.

Mr. Pearlman seemed puzzled by the request. Nevertheless, he said, "Wait here," and left the office.

He was gone half an hour.

"I've a surprise for you," he said upon his return. "All three boys had tests scheduled today."

"In what subjects?" inquired Encyclopedia.

"Jim Carnes took a history test at eight," said Mr. Pearlman. "Chuck Mitchell took a spelling test at nine. Right now, Bert Fenton is taking a test in Spanish."

Mr. Pearlman paused and regarded Encyclopedia questioningly.

"If you think you know who poisoned Corby's skunk, I wish you'd tell me his name," he said.

"And me!" exclaimed Sally.

"Well, then," said Encyclopedia. "I think the guilty boy is . . ."

WHO?

(Turn to page 95 for the solution to The Case of the Pet Skunk.)

The Case of the Seven-Foot Driver

Baxter Cronkmeyer wobbled stiffly up to the Brown Detective Agency. He wore a paper moustache and a skirt made of old curtains that hung to the ground.

"Hi," he said, ducking under the door frame.

Baxter was a growing boy. Still, it was hard to believe that he'd grown *three feet* since Encyclopedia had seen him last.

The boy detective stood up, startled. His eyes were on a level with Baxter's knees.

"Baxter!" gasped Sally. "What have you been eating? Vitamins or curtain rods?"

"Shook you up, eh?" said Baxter gleefully.

Grinning, he untied the rope at his waist. The curtains fell to the floor, showing the reason for his jiffy growth. He was standing on stilts.

"I'm going to scare Jack Hightower pop-eyed," he declared.

The name gave Encyclopedia gooseflesh. Jack Hightower was eighteen. He had a temper as short as he was long, which was seven feet. *He* usually did the scaring.

"What makes you so mad at Jack?" inquired Sally.

"Reckless driving," snorted Baxter.

He explained. Two hours ago he had been riding his yellow bike when Jack drove his car around the corner at high speed. Baxter barely had time to jump clear.

"I wasn't hurt," said Baxter. "But Jack ran over my bike. It looks like mashed noodles."

"Are you sure it was Jack?" asked Sally.

"Farnsworth Grant saw him," said Baxter.

"But Farnsworth won't come with me to Jack's house."

"The fraidy cat!" said Sally.

"I'm on my way to speak with Jack," said Baxter. "That's why I'm dressed like this. Jack hasn't looked *up* at anyone since he was thirteen. When he sees me, he'll be glad to pay for my bike."

"You don't weigh a hundred pounds," Sally said. "Jack weighs two hundred and forty. Get him mad, and he'll pull your curtain-tails and sling you over the roof. Then he'll stuff the stilts up your nose."

Baxter winced. "That's why I stopped here," he said. He laid twenty-five cents on the gasoline can beside Encyclopedia. "If I don't fool Jack, I may need lots of help."

Encyclopedia considered the twenty-five cents. He also considered how it must feel to be stepped on by two hundred and forty pounds, or even leaned on. His fast brain worked on a way to wiggle out of the case.

He said weakly, "You're not sure it was Jack. *You* didn't see him behind the wheel."

"No, but I saw it was Jack's green car," replied Baxter.

"We'll take the case," said Sally, glancing reproachfully at Encyclopedia. "First, we'll have to do something about your getup. You look more like a French window than a giant."

The two detectives got busy. Sally pinned the curtains to form trousers. Encyclopedia stuffed a clothes hanger under Baxter's shirt to widen his shoulders.

"You've got the shortest arms of anybody over eight feet tall," said the boy detective. "Keep your hands in your pockets, and Jack won't notice. Let's go."

The Hightowers lived three blocks away. After walking a block, Baxter seemed to lose heart. "I can't go through with it," he whined.

He plodded to a halt beside a small girl. She

"Zowie!" Baxter yelped excitedly. "I scared her!"

jumped off her tricycle and fled into the house crying.

"Zowie!" Baxter yelped excitedly. "I scared her! I can do the same to Jack, the dirty hit-and-run artist!"

Encyclopedia saw Jack's green car parked in the driveway of his house. Jack loomed by the garage. He stared at the three children.

"Who's the little dude on stilts?" he asked.

"*He means me*," whimpered Baxter. "Let's get out of here. I've got too much bone in my head and not enough in my back."

Desperately, Encyclopedia signaled Sally to retreat. It was too late. She had her fists planted on her hips and her jaw stuck out.

"You nearly killed Baxter Cronkmeyer this morning with your reckless driving," she said to Jack. "And you ran over his bike and ruined it. We've come to collect for a new one!"

"You bucking for a stretcher or something?" growled Jack. "I wasn't in my car this morning.

My sister was the only one to use it today. She's a careful driver."

He turned toward the house.

"Alice," he called. "Come out here a minute."

Alice Hightower was seventeen, but hardly taller than Sally. Jack told her what was going on.

"I wasn't in the car today," he said to her. "You were the only person to drive it. Isn't that correct?"

Alice looked frightened. "Y-yes," she stammered.

"Now, do I look like my sister?" demanded Jack. "Anyone who mistakes me for Alice ought to adopt a seeing-eye dog. You're accusing the wrong man."

He opened the door of his car and slipped comfortably behind the wheel without bothering to use the seat belt. He started the engine.

"I've got an appointment," he said, slamming the door. "It's with a man who thinks I'll be the next heavyweight boxing champion of the world."

"You come back and pay for Baxter's bike!" screamed Sally. "Encyclopedia, don't let him get away with it!"

Encyclopedia's legs felt like rubber bands, and the breeze was twanging them. Nevertheless, he shouted, "You're lying, Jack. You drove over Baxter's bike!"

WHAT WAS THE PROOF?

(*Turn to page 96 for the solution to The Case of the Seven-Foot Driver.*)

Solution to *The Case of the Stolen Money*

After stealing the money and hiding it in his own house, Mr. Aukland returned to the Richters' house with rope.

He called the police, claiming the rope had been used by two thieves to tie him; before he could free himself the thieves got away with the money.

However, he claimed to have seen them clearly before they knocked off his glasses.

Impossible!

Entering a house heated to seventy degrees—a comfortable temperature—from the outdoors on a freezing day, Mr. Aukland could not have seen anything.

His eyeglasses would have been steamed over!

Thanks to Encyclopedia, Mr. Aukland confessed.

Solution to *The Case of the Talking House*

When Scoop thought the house bit him, he dropped his money and ran.

Bugs didn't have a chance to hide. He knew Scoop had seen him as he raced to Encyclopedia for help.

The Tigers' leader wanted the detective to find the money and so believe him innocent. Therefore, he put the half dollar on top of the dollar bill to weigh it down in the sand.

That was his mistake!

When a coin and a bill are dropped, the coin lands first. The bill floats down and lands on top of the coin, not underneath it.

Trapped by his own mistake, Bugs admitted that he had pretended to be the house and had asked Scoop for money.

Solution to *The Case of the Two-Timers*

Bugs used Lefty to help him get even with the two detectives.

While Bugs and Officer Hall watched from the dress shop, Lefty paid Encyclopedia twenty-five cents and then five dollars.

To Officer Hall, it looked as if Lefty were paying the fee for setting his watch and then buying the rights to charge others.

But Lefty could not have been setting his watch. He was so nervous he used his left hand.

If you set your watch with your left hand, you will be holding it *upside down!*

When Encyclopedia pointed out Lefty's slip to Officer Hall, the policeman realized Lefty and Bugs had faked the whole scene.

Solution to *The Case of the False Teeth*

Duke had to think fast in order to explain the bite in his ear.

So he said he had chased the newspaper ads into the ocean, stumbled, and was bitten by a crab.

But he forgot about the wind.

It was blowing in from the ocean all the time Encyclopedia and Sally were on the beach.

Thus, the pieces of newspapers would have blown inland, not into the ocean *against the wind*.

Caught by his own lie, Duke admitted stealing the jar of teeth in order to collect the rewards. Rocky Graham had taken the jar to the Tigers' clubhouse.

Freddy got back his teeth.

Solution to *The Case of the Skin Diver*

Marlin claimed he had been skin diving and had come ashore to ask Trisk to stop scaling stones into the water.

If he spoke the truth, the water should have wiped out his part. Yet he had a part—even though he had no comb with him!

From that clue, Sally reasoned out what had taken place.

Marlin felt that since he was naked and he wore a face mask when he stole the earring from Trisk, he could not be recognized as the thief—except for one thing. His hair was always parted down the middle.

So, after putting on his clothes, he parted his hair on the side. Then he hid the comb and the earring in the bushes when he saw Encyclopedia, Sally, and Trisk approach. Without the comb, he couldn't be accused of having changed the part. He planned to come back for the earring later.

Solution to *The Case of the Barefoot Thieves*

Pete and Stingy Stetson had taken off their shoes and socks in the truck in order to walk quietly. They had entered and left the building by walking along the white stripes of the parking lot.

As they left, Tyrone Taylor had sat down under the tree. The brothers did not see him. But he saw them—from the waist up—walking back to the truck.

Encyclopedia realized the brothers had not walked along the white stripe just for fun. It was a hot day, remember?

The blacktop burned their bare feet. So they had walked along the white strip—which was cooler.

Faced with the proof revealed by Tyrone's sharp eyes and Encyclopedia's sharp brain, the Stetson brothers confessed.

Solution to *The Case of the Dog-Paddle Derby*

Encyclopedia meant that in Canada an Imperial gallon holds five quarts. But in the United States, a gallon holds four quarts.

To throw suspicion off himself, Puddinghead claimed he made only one trip to the shed to fill the one-gallon gasoline can before the final race.

Impossible! He could not have filled five one-quart bowls to the top with a gallon of water.

He really made two trips. On the second trip, he put the knockout drops into the can and filled the fifth bowl—the one Rags drank from.

Horace Cushing was in on the scheme. He made sure Rags, the favorite, was placed before the proper bowl.

Because of Encyclopedia's quick brain, the race was rerun the next week, and Rags won.

Solution to *The Case of the Broken Globe*

Gene Dickman had written only one word to describe each picture in the test: NOON, SEES, RADAR, LEVEL, REPAPER, and SOLOS.

The six words were the clue.

Each was a palindrome; that is, a word that reads the same backward and forward.

Two students, Encyclopedia saw, had names that were palindromes. They were ANNA McGill and Robert—BOB—Mason.

The next day Mr. Morton questioned only Anna and Bob about the broken globe. They thought he had positive proof of their guilt, so they confessed.

After he had left the classroom during the test, they had clowned around and had accidentally knocked over the globe.

Solution to *The Case of the Pet Skunk*

As Encyclopedia guessed, the slip of paper had fallen out of the guilty boy's pocket when he took out the bottle of poison.

On the paper was typed: "In order to succeed you have to proceed to exceed."

The sentence makes good sense only as a way of remembering the words in the English language that end in "ceed." Many words end in "cede," which sounds like "ceed." But only three words—succeed, proceed, and exceed—end in "ceed."

Encyclopedia realized the guilty boy had written down the sentence to help him remember the three words—in preparation for a spelling test.

Thus, the boy was Chuck Mitchell.

Solution to *The Case of the Seven-Foot Driver*

Alice lied in order to help her brother.

The difference in their sizes gave Encyclopedia the clue.

Alice was hardly taller than Sally. Jack was seven feet.

But he forgot about the seat.

He settled into it comfortably.

Had Alice really driven the car last, he would have had to move the seat back to fit his long legs.

Proved guilty by his own actions, Jack bought Baxter a new bike.